NOBODY STOLE THE PIE

Nobody

ILLUSTRATIONS BY
FERNANDO KRAHN

Stole the Pie

STORY BY
SONIA LEVITIN

HBJ
HARCOURT
BRACE
JOVANOVICH
NEW YORK AND LONDON

To my family

Requests for permission to make copies of
any part of the work should be mailed to:
Permissions, Harcourt Brace Jovanovich, Inc.,
757 Third Avenue, New York, New York 10017

Printed in the United States of America

Library of Congress Cataloging in Publication Data
Levitin, Sonia, 1934–
Nobody stole the pie.
Summary: The annual lollyberry festival in Little
Digby is marred because everybody sneaks a little
taste of the pie they are all to share, thinking
there will be plenty left for the celebration.
[1. Pies—Fiction] I. Krahn, Fernando. II. Title.
PZ7.L58Nl   [E]   79–90032
ISBN 0–15–257469–7   ISBN 0–15–665959–X pbk.

Set in VIP Aster
First Edition
B C D E

In a distant town called Little Digby,
there grew a wonderful lollyberry tree.

Was it magic? you will want to know. I will have to answer no, not magic in the way of granting wishes or producing ice-cream cones instead of flowers. But it was a *very good* tree. And perhaps there is a kind of magic about being always, steadily, reliably *very good*.

The lollyberry tree grew in the center of town, very near the City Hall, where the Mayor, who was wise, worked to keep things in order.

The townsfolk of Little Digby took good care of their lollyberry tree. So, each spring it bore beautiful blossoms of pink and purple. Each summer there appeared the luscious and juicy, sweet and tangy lollyberries. They were delicious.

The lollyberry tree gave berries enough for everyone. It had been decided long ago that the berries would be shared. The sharing was a happy festival.

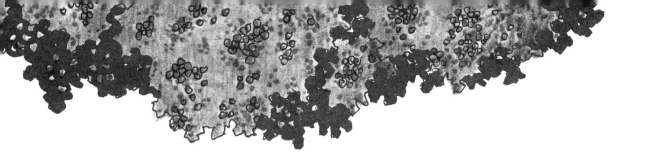

Each year at summer's end, the
pickers picked the berries and put them
into huge vats. Then the washers
washed the berries. And then the bakers
began the merriest, most delightful
work of the year; they baked a
tremendous lollyberry pie.

They mixed it in special mixing bowls with special spoons. They placed it in a special pan. They baked it in a special oven. And when it was done, ten bakers hoisted the pie up onto the platform outside the City Hall, where it stood all day to cool.

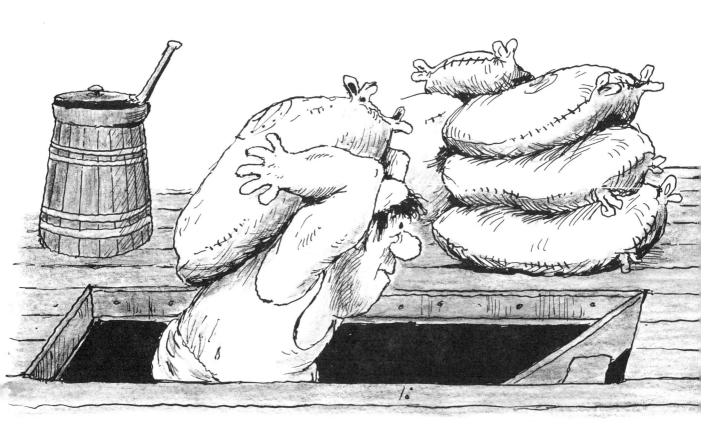

From the street nobody could see
the pie, except for the very rim. But
everybody in Little Digby could smell it.
Mouths watered and hearts quickened,
joyful for the evening, when all would

meet in the town square and the Mayor
would cut the pie and everybody would
have a share. Then the music and the
dancing and the merriment would last
throughout the night.

All day the children and the parents, the young people and the old, sang this song of gladness:

> *"Oh, the lollyberry tree,*
> *Enough for you and me.*
> *Oh, the lollyberry pie,*
> *Enough for you and I!"*

. . . which isn't proper grammar, but the Mayor, wisely, did not correct them. Sometimes the feeling is more important than the word.

Now, in this particular year, after the berries had been picked and washed, after the pie had been mixed and baked and set high upon the platform to cool, something happened.

It was a very small thing. A bird flew over the pie, dipped his beak down, and pulled out a berry—a single berry from the lollyberry pie.

It was delicious.

A cat, stalking the bird,
had perched on the platform.
She saw the bird fly with the
beautiful berry dripping
from his mouth.
She stuck her paw onto
the edge of the pie,
picked a bit of crust,
and considered it delicious.
She took a little more.

The chief of all the bakers observed the cat eating the crust, decided no harm was done, and plucked up the crumbs that had fallen to the side.

The next baker in line, watching from behind the doorway, saw the chief smacking his lips and decided: "If the chief can do it, why can't I?" He stood up on tiptoe and picked out a bit of pie. It was delicious.

He went back to work, humming a tune, thinking the words:

"A little bit, a little bit, a little bit won't hurt."

The next baker after the next baker after the next baker took a taste, and so on, until all ten bakers had eaten and sung to themselves:

"A little bit, a little bit, a little bit won't hurt."

Pursy Nurse came by. She had had a hard night nursing and cursing. She was very tired. From the corner of her tired old eye she saw the last baker in line helping himself to a piece of pie. "Humpf," she thought, "I was up all night. I am too tired. A little nibble of pie would perk me up."

She strained on tiptoe, reached over the rim, and took out a teensy-weensy piece of pie. It was delicious. And she hobbled home, singing to herself:

"A little bit, a little bit, a little bit won't hurt."

Now came the poor patient
whom the nurse had tended
that night, groaning over the pain in his back. He noticed
the nurse nibbling the pie and thought, "Why not? I have
suffered pain and deserve a special treat. Nobody will care."

He lifted himself high, stretched out his cane, and
caught himself a fine hunk of pie. It was delicious.
He limped on, muttering:

"A little bit, a little bit, a little bit won't hurt."

Now, the wife of the patient was on her way to market.

She was also feeling sorry for herself. Marketing was the man's job. She had enough to do. She saw a dribble of lollyberry running down her husband's beard and said to herself, "Why not? I did extra work. I ought to get extra pie. Nobody will know." She stood upon a fine flat stone, reached up, and brought down a lovely helping of pie. It was delicious. She walked on to market saying to herself:

"A little bit, a little bit, a little bit won't hurt."

Next came her
children, all six,
and they saw that
Mama had enjoyed
the pie, and they
said to themselves
and to each other,
"If it is good for Mama,
it is good for us." The
six of them formed a
ladder, taking turns
being on top, and each
reached over and
scooped out a piece
of pie. It was delicious.
Then they all ran off down the lane shouting together:

"A little bit, a little bit, a little bit won't hurt."

And so all the day long as people came by, they took and they snatched and they ate from that pie. And some came from far away, not from the town.

And many ate more than anyone should.
And sad to say, those good folks who had
kept to their work had nothing that day
but to look forward to the night.

And
so the day
moved on into
dusk. All the towns-
folk met outside the
City Hall. They gathered
all around the lollyberry
tree waiting and smacking
their lips. All eyes rose
when their Mayor came
forth and rang the big
bell that signaled the
start of the Lolly-
berry Festival.
The Mayor
wisely

made a
short speech
about what a truly
wonderful town, what
a wonderful City Hall,
what a wonderful tree,
what a wonderful pie it
was. Then he ordered the
ten bakers to bring down
the pie and to set it on
the long, long table
where it would be
cut and divided
and shared.
They did
so.

And when at last the pie had been set down upon the table, a great silence fell over the multitude, and then a great gasp rose from them all. The pie, the beautiful, wonderful, plump, and delicious lollyberry pie was gone—all except for a single piece stuck onto the very edge of the rim.

For a few moments
the Mayor said nothing.
Then he looked out
over the crowd,
raised both hands
for attention,
and asked in
a loud voice,

"Who has stolen the pie?"

There was silence.
Then came a murmuring,
like the buzzing of
a thousand bees.
People shrugged.
They shook their heads.
They gazed about.
Each said to himself,
"Who could have done
such a bad deed?

"It's one thing to
take a taste, a speck,
a piece—but the *whole pie!*
That is a terrible crime."

Loudly the Mayor declared it.
"Somebody stole the pie!"

The townsfolk looked at each other.

"Not I."

"Not I."

"Not I."

The Mayor gazed around. He pulled himself up tall. Then he said with a smile, "It is clear that if nobody stole the pie, it must still be here. And since it is here, we shall proceed. As is our custom, the Mayor shall have the very first piece."

Whereupon the Mayor
reached over,
took up the one,
the last, the
only piece of pie,
and ate it up,
every crumb.

That night there was no dancing or
singing or merriment. The townsfolk
went home, sorely puzzled, for if nobody
stole the pie, then certainly it still had
to be there. But if it had been there,
why were they feeling so oddly, so
sadly, so awfully empty?

The Mayor, wisely, did not tell them.
Someday, he thought, they would figure
it out for themselves. He knew they
would understand that *everybody*
stole the pie.